Rain Makes a Farm

Written by **Daniel Collins**   Illustrated by **Van Hai Van**

Layout by **Brandon Duncan**

Copyright 2024 Daniel Collins

In loving memory of
Chace, Chickpea, and Uncle Joe

Hi, my name is Nova. My best friend's name is Rain. I suppose you'd call her my human Mom, since she takes care of me.

My Mom loves her farm! She grows plants, herbs, and even food that she eats. Not me—tomatoes are yuck! Although I do enjoy blueberries as a snack sometimes! We have strawberries, kale, lettuce, pear trees, lavender, garlic, and even dandelions (who knew those were good for people?).

Meet Firefly! She lays what my Mom calls "the most delicious eggs!" which we get to sell at the farmer's market. She tills the ground with her beak and fertilizes the grass.

Firefly has other friends that help her as well. While I cannot remember all of their names, Mom moves them around the farm to prepare the soil for new plants.

This black and white fur ball is Sora. I am not a big fan, but I tolerate her to make Mom happy. She does have a specific responsibility, though. She keeps the mice, rats, and other vermin away from the house and chicken coop! Even though I don't like to admit it, she excels at this task.

However, Mom "rules the roost." When she is not busy caring for one of us animals, I watch her lovingly plant so many plants. She always says the same thing after she gets done: "Now all we need is some rain. Rain makes a farm!"

Made in United States
Orlando, FL
22 September 2025